Domino

Jess

Tommy

Seal

Peggy

Max

EKKU

First published in 2001 in Great Britain by

GULLANE
CHILDREN'S BOOKS

Winchester House, 259-269

Old Marylebone Road, London NW1 5XJ

1 3 5 7 9 10 8 6 4 2

Illustrations © Jane Cabrera 2001

A CIP record for this title is available

from the British Library.

The right of Jane Cabrera to be identified

as the illustrator of this work has been

asserted by her in accordance

with the Copyright, Designs,

and Patents Act, 1988.

ISBN 1-86233-340-8

Printed and bound in Belgium

For Paula

Jane Cabrera

Old Mother Hubbard

GULLANE
CHILDREN'S BOOKS

Old Mother Hubbard
went to the cupboard

But when she got there, the cupboard was bare, and so the poor dog had none

She went to
the tailor's

to buy him
a coat

But when she came back, he was riding a goat

She went to
the hatter's

to buy him
a hat

But when she
came back,
he was washing
the cat

She went to
the barber's

to buy him
a wig

She went to
the cobbler's

to buy him
some shoes

But when
she came back,
he was reading
the news

Then the dame made a curtsy,

The dog
made a bow